ASHA'S MUMS

women's
PRESS

by Rosamund Elwin
& Michele Paulse

Illustrated by
Dawn Lee

My class has been talking all week about the trip we're going to take to the Science Centre. Some of the children like Terrence and Elsie have already been there.

"My favourite part is the machine that makes your hair stand up like a porcupine!" Terrence exclaimed. "And mine is a bicycle that tests your strength when you pedal it," Elsie added.

My teacher Ms. Samuels gave us a form to take home. Our parents had to fill it out and sign it so that we would have permission to go on the trip. I gave it back to her the next day.

Just before break she asked to see me. She wanted to know which of the names on the form was my mum's.

I said, "Both."
"It can't be both. You can't have two mums," she said briskly.
"But I do! My brother and I have two mums," I protested.
Coreen and Judi were listening to me.
"Take the form back home and have it filled out correctly,"
Ms. Samuels said.
"You can't go on the trip if it isn't." She also gave me a note.

I went to my desk. "What did Ms. Samuels want?"
Rita whispered. Rita and I are best friends.
"She doesn't believe I have two mums. I have to
take my form back home and have it filled out
right or I can't go to the Science Centre."
Then the bell rang for recess.
Rita, Diane and I went to play jump rope.

When I got home I gave my mum Alice the form and
the note. "The trip is only two days away. I can't go if
the form isn't filled out right. All the kids are going to go
without me." Mum Alice gave me a big hug and a kiss
and said, "Don't worry about it Asha, the form is filled
out right. We'll go see your teacher and talk with her."
I felt better because I knew they would.

Before I went to sleep that night, I thought about the fun Rita and Diane and the other kids would have at the Science Centre. Would I be going with them too? "If I don't get to go I'm not ever going back to school again," I promised.

The next day I helped Ms. Samuels set up for Show and Tell. I got a big sheet of drawing paper and drew a picture of my family and the building we live in. I put in some bricks, a smiling sun, and big fluffy clouds. I drew Mark and our mummies Sara and Alice.

When my turn came to talk about my drawing
I said, "This is my brother Mark and my mummies
and me. We're on our way to the Science Centre."

Coreen said "How come you've got two mummies?"
"Because I do," I said.
"You can't have two mummies," Judi insisted.
"Yes she can," Rita said turning around in her seat.
"Just like you can have two aunts, and two daddies and
two grandmas," yelled Diane from across the room.
Diane likes to yell.

"See," I said to Coreen.
"My mum and dad said you can't have two mothers living together. My dad says it's bad," Coreen insisted.
"It's not bad. My mummies said we're a family because we live together and love each other," I said.
"But how come you have two?" Judi asked.

Before I could answer Terrence said to Ms. Samuels,
"Is it wrong to have two mummies?"
"Well..." Ms. Samuels began but Diane yelled, "It's not
wrong if they're nice to you and if you like them."

Everyone began talking at once. It got really noisy.
The bell rang and I didn't get to finish my story.

After school both Sara and Alice came to pick me up. I told them what happened in class. "We talked to your teacher while you were at gym," Sara said. Do I get to go to the Science Centre tomorrow? Do I get to look like a porcupine? Does she believe I have two mummies?" I shouted all at once. "One question at a time," Alice laughed. "Yes you can go to the Science Centre."

"Yeepee!" I yelled, skipping up and down. "Thanks mum,"
I said to Alice and kissed her cheeks. "Thanks mum," I said
to Sara and kissed her cheeks. "Gee, you're welcome," they
said, laughing as I skipped ahead of them. "Don't you want
to know the answer to your other question?" Sara asked.
I did but not right then.

I was so excited about the trip today, I was up before everyone else. I put on my favorite red sweat suit and my yellow
and white sneakers with the hearts on the side.

Alice took me to class. When Terrence and Diane saw her they ran up to her. "Which mummy are you?" Terrence asked. "Mummy number one," she said smiling.

The trip to the Science Centre was lots and lots of fun. I even got to look like a porcupine.

When Sara picked me up after school, Terrence, Diane, and
Coreen asked together, "Whiiiich mummyyy arrrre yooou?"
"Mummy number one," Sara answered.
Everybody laughed.